# Snakes in the Grass

**Published by Ladybird Books Ltd 2012**
A Penguin Company
Penguin Books Ltd, 80 Strand, London, WC2R 0RL, UK
Penguin Books Australia Ltd, Camberwell, Victoria, Australia
Penguin Group (NZ), 67 Apollo Drive, Rosedale, Auckland
0632, New Zealand (a division of Pearson New Zealand Ltd)

"Cold Reception", "The Bravest Ninja of All",
"Snakes in the Grass" and "The Keys to Victory"
written by Greg Farshtey

LEGO, the LEGO logo, the Brick and Knob configurations and the Minifigure
are trademarks of the LEGO Group.
©2012 The LEGO Group.

 Produced by AMEET Sp. z o.o.
under license from the LEGO Group.

AMEET Sp. z o.o.,
Przybyszewskiego 176/178, 93-120 Łódź – Poland
ameet@ameet.com.pl
www.ameet.pl

Penguin Books Ltd, 80 Strand, London, WC2R 0RL, UK
Please keep the Penguin Books Ltd address for future reference.
www.LEGO.com

ISBN: 9781409313984
001 - 10 9 8 7 6 5 4 3 2 1
Printed in Poland

Item name: LEGO® Ninjago. Snakes in the Grass / The Bravest Ninja of All
Series: LNR
Item number: LNR 6/LNR 5
Batch: 01/GB

# Contents

# Bad Alliesss

The new menace to Ninjago put my young Masters of Spinjitzu on alert. Lloyd Garmadon's snake army brought fear and chaos to our world, so Cole, Kai, Jay and Zane did their best to stop them. It was not long before Lloyd discovered the bitter taste of betrayal. The Hypnobrai turned against him and he had to escape. Planning his revenge, he sought new allies. Fate and a map stolen from the Hypnobrai brought him to the long-forgotten lair of another snake tribe...

# Venomous Bite

Whatever mischief the Fangpyre had got up to in the past, there was at least one good reason for locking them up in an impenetrable tomb – their venomous bite! A Fangpyre's bite can transform any living or non-living thing into a ferocious, snake-like creature! Hoping to lead those dreadful snakes against the deceitful Hypnobrai, my reckless nephew released the Fangpyre from their confinement. Little did he know that instead of fighting each other, the two evil snake tribes would join forces.

# Snakes in the Grass

Kai awoke to a strange noise. It sounded like the air escaping from a tyre, but the Ninja of Fire knew it was nothing as innocent as that. It had to be

the hissing of a snake.

He sprang to his feet and grabbed the Dragon Sword of Fire. If the Fangpyre were making another attempt to sneak into the ninja camp, he would invite them to a barbecue they would never forget.

Peering into the darkness, he saw a tall figure moving. As the shadowy presence

came closer, Kai relaxed. It was Sensei Wu on one of his usual midnight walks. The Sensei nodded in his direction.

"A beautiful night," the old man said.

"I guess," said Kai. "But I thought I heard something moving around ... maybe a snake."

Sensei Wu chuckled. "There are no sssssnakes here," he replied. "You sssshould get ssssome ssssleep."

Kai jumped backwards and raised his sword. The fire from the blade lit up the surrounding area. Now the ninja could see that Sensei Wu's skin was covered with scales.

"No!" yelled Kai. "The Fangpyre got to you! You're one of them!"

"Calm down," Sensei Wu said softly. "The Sssserpentine are our friends. I am older and ssssmarter than you, Kai, you sssshould pay attention to what I ssssay."

"Try paying attention to this!" said Kai, as he swung his flaming sword.

To the ninja's amazement, the Sensei caught the blade in his hand. Even though the sword was burning, the Sensei did not cry out. It was as if he didn't even feel the fire.

"Okay, I get it," said Kai. "Snake-Sensei is too much for me to handle. Good thing I have friends. Cole! Zane! Jay!"

Behind him, Kai could hear his three friends running to help him. Despite the terrible circumstances, he felt calm. There was no danger his ninja team couldn't handle as long as they were together.

Cole spoke first. "What's the ssssituation, Kai?"

Kai felt his stomach drop.

"Probably just ssssomething he ate," said Jay.

"That would make no ssssense," Zane said. "Why would his choice of dinner cause him to cry out? Unless, of course, we are out of sssssnake food."

Kai did a backflip from a standing start, soaring over the heads of the other three ninja and landing behind them. When they turned to face him, he saw that they too now looked like snake-men.

"The Fangpyre," said Kai. "They must have snuck in during the night and turned you all into snakes."

"It's really not sssso bad," said Cole.

"We're sssstronger now," Jay put in. "Faster, too."

"Plus, we no longer need to waste time fighting for justice," said Zane. "Now we just sssserve the Sssserpentine."

"It's ssssimply the best," said a familiar voice. A moment later, Nya, Kai's sister, slithered into view. She had become a snake too!

"Now it is time for you to join the Fangpyre," Sensei Wu said, advancing on Kai. The others followed behind him, hissing angrily.

Kai didn't know what to do. If he fought, he might hurt his friends, and he knew they weren't responsible for what had happened to them. Yet they were part of the Serpentine now, and so a threat to all humans, and especially to him.

*Maybe if I run to the village nearby, I can get help,* Kai thought. *If we can just capture Sensei Wu and the others, maybe there is some way to cure them.*

Kai slashed downward with his sword, creating a flaming trench in the ground. The smoke and the fire blinded his former friends for a moment, giving Kai time to dash off into the woods.

He ran as fast as he could until he saw the campfires of the village up ahead. Although it was late, there seemed to be plenty of people out in the town square. With luck, they would be brave and strong enough to fight ninja snakes.

Kai raced into the village . . . then skidded to a halt in the dirt. The villagers had turned as one to look at him – and they were all Fangpyre too! He was too late.

The Ninja of Fire turned to see Sensei Wu and the others coming toward him. He was trapped. Soon, they would turn him into a snake like them and he would be fighting for the Serpentine. He closed his eyes so he wouldn't have to see what was about to happen.

A moment later, Kai opened his eyes. Crouched above him were Jay, Zane, Cole, Nya and Sensei Wu, all looking perfectly normal.

"Hey, you were yelling in your sleep," said Jay. "We thought we'd better check on you."

"A dream," Kai said, relieved. "It was all just a bad dream. Except . . . the Fangpyre are real, and so is what they can do, right?"

"Very real," said Sensei Wu.

"Then it could still happen," Kai said, getting up and grabbing his sword. "But not if we stop them first. Tomorrow, guys, we are going to smash the Fangpyre once and for all."

# Snake Venom

*What is often thought to be bad for you is not always entirely bad – and not just in Ninjago. Take the snakes' most dangerous weapon, for example...*

**1.** Venom is modified snake saliva. It is produced in venom glands – small sacs located in the snake's head behind the eyes – and usually released through long, hollow fangs when the snake bites.

**2.** Venom can be very dangerous when it gets into the blood of a bitten victim. The only cure for illness caused by a snake bite is *antivenin*, made from...snake venom.

**3.** Some animals – like opossums, mongooses or hedgehogs – are immune to certain venoms. Humans are not.

**4.** Snake venom is also used to produce medicines for treating various illnesses, such as high blood pressure or epilepsy. Until the 1940s, it was one of the main ingredients of many painkillers.

**5.** Snakes keep producing venom for as long as they live. In order to obtain this precious substance, venomous snakes are caught and bred on snake farms.

**6.** Venom is "milked" from snake fangs by squeezing the venom sacs and forcing the release of the venom into a small container. It is then frozen and stored in proper conditions before further processing.

## Sensei Wu asks

*It sounds unbelievable, but not every bite from a venomous snake will inject venom. True or false?*

**Answer:** True. Snakes with fangs located at the back of the jaw – like the African boomslang – may fail to inject venom when they bite. Sometimes the fangs simply do not reach the victim at all. However, every snake bite should be seen by a doctor and treated very seriously!

# The Prophecy

"One ninja will rise above the others and become the Green Ninja ... the ninja destined to defeat the dark lord." This is what Kai, Jay, Cole and Zane read from an ancient scroll that accidentally fell into their hands. Who were the words referring to? At that time, even I did not know — only the future held the answer. Yet, upon learning of the prophecy, the boys vigorously resumed their arduous training. Each of them believed that he would soon prove to be the mysterious warrior, who would ultimately free Ninjago from evil.

# The Keys to Victory

Kai raised his sword, a smile on his lips as he eyed his foe. This was a fight he couldn't lose. When it was over, his opponent would be on the ground begging for mercy.

He swung his weapon. Jay easily sidestepped the blow and responded with his Nunchucks of Lightning. They wrapped around Kai's sword and sent a jolt of electricity down the blade and into Kai's arm, knocking the Ninja of Fire flat.

"Ha!" said Jay. "I knew you would fall for that trick – and I do mean *fall*."

Kai stood up and brushed the dirt from his ninja robes. Taking off the protective mask he wore for training sessions, he said, "Okay, so you won three, and I won three. Want to go again?"

Jay pointed past Kai. "Sure. But you might want to check that out first."

Kai turned around. He saw his sister, Nya, practising her kicks with a training dummy. Not for the first time, Kai was amazed at her fighting skills ... though of course, he would never tell her that. Instead, he walked over to where she was working out and said, "What do you think you're doing?"

"Practising," she said, in between kicks, "to be a ninja."

"You can't be a ninja," Kai answered. "You're a girl!"

"I'm as fast as you are. I'm as good in a fight as you are," Nya answered. "And I'm *way* smarter than you are, brother. One of these days, Sensei Wu will make me a ninja."

"Right, sure, the day he makes Lloyd Garmadon a ninja, too," Kai snorted.

"If you two are done arguing, we have something important to talk about," said Cole. He was carrying a piece of parchment in his hands. Zane and Jay were following behind him. "Zane says there are Fangpyre up in the hills. We need to go and find them."

"That's easier said than done," Zane added. "The pathway is treacherous and we don't have enough mules for the four of us. Also, the animals are slow. We would never be able to evade a Fangpyre attack while riding them."

"You guys worry too much," said Jay. "Don't you know I always have the answer?"

Jay led his friends to a corner of the camp. Something big was covered by a sheet. With a smile, Jay yanked the sheet off to reveal four gleaming motorcycles. Each one of them had a special plate on the front featuring one of the four elements the ninja represented: lightning, fire, ice and earth. Zane, Kai and Cole all gasped in amazement at the incredible vehicles.

"I built them in my spare time," said Jay, proudly. "I thought we might need them some day."

"Sure," said Nya, turning to walk away from him. "You thought you might need four of them … you knew you wouldn't need five."

"Nya, wait!" said Jay, starting after her. "I didn't mean anything by it. It's just … we're the team, you know? And you're … ."

"I'm just along for the ride," Nya snapped, "but not on one of your cycles."

Jay walked back to the others, feeling sad and angry at the same time. Sometimes, Nya was hard to understand. Kai patted him on the back.

"Don't worry about it," said the Ninja of Fire. "She'll calm down. She always does. But … you built these? Really? I mean, I know you tinker with things, but … wow."

"Yes, from scratch," said Jay, managing a smile. "A few nuts here, a few bolts there, a couple of wheels, and you've got a cycle."

"It's getting dark," said Cole. "We'll start searching for the Fangpyre in the morning. Jay, take first watch. The rest of you, get some sleep."

Jay did his best to stay vigilant that night, but his thoughts kept turning to Nya. Was she really angry at him? They had just started to become close friends, and he would hate to think that friendship had been damaged. Still, it would be much too dangerous for her to go searching for Fangpyre without ninja training.

So absorbed was Jay in his thoughts and worries that he never heard a Fangpyre slip into camp that night...

As soon as dawn broke, the four ninja were ready to mount their new cycles and head into the mountains. Nya was nowhere to be found. Kai suggested she was probably out for a walk and would be back soon.

"Let's ride!" said Kai, smiling as he got on his bike. The other ninja followed. As soon as they turned the keys in the ignition, the engines roared into life.

Then something very strange happened. Before Kai even put his hands on the handlebars, the front wheel

began to turn. Impossibly, it turned all the way around, as if the bike was made of rubber. The headlights looked like snake eyes and the metal frame above the front tyre now had a mouth with steel fangs. The cycle snapped at Kai and the ninja jumped back, landing on the ground.

"What's wrong with this thing?" Kai shouted, dodging out of the way at the last moment as the motorcycle tried to run him down.

The other ninja had troubles of their own. Their cycles had come to life as well, hissing and spitting and trying to sink their teeth into the heroes. Cole, Jay and Zane ducked and dodged, but found their strongest blows did little more than dent the metal cycles.

"You built these a little too well," Zane said to Jay, as he avoided another strike from the cycle.

"Quality," Jay answered, leaping over his bike. "It's all about quality."

"It's the Fangpyre" said Cole, using a branch to fend off his cycle. "They must have got into the camp last night and bitten the motorcycles. Sensei Wu said they can even turn machinery into serpents."

Kai's bike charged. He caught it by the handlebars and used the cycle's momentum to flip it over his hip and slam it onto the ground. The bike writhed and lashed out with its rear wheel, knocking Kai backwards.

Nearby, Jay had what he thought was a great idea. He whirled the Nunchucks of Lightning above his head and then hit his cycle with it. A massive jolt of electricity hit the bike. Yet instead of stopping it, the vehicle actually seemed to get stronger.

"It's feeding on the power!" yelled Zane. "We'll have to think of something else."

"I'm – yikes! – open to suggestions," Jay said, narrowly avoiding being bitten by the bike. He wasn't sure if the motorcycle's fangs could turn him into a snake or not, but he wasn't interested in testing the theory, either.

"Go for the headlights!" Cole yelled "Maybe we can blind them."

Kai had managed to get on his cycle. It was bucking like a horse, trying to throw him off. "Next time, make us something a little safer, Jay," he said. "Like snowshoes."

His cycle abruptly stopped short, hurling Kai over the handlebars and onto the ground. He lay there, stunned, unable to defend himself as the bike closed in.

Jay dove in Kai's direction, grabbing his friend and pulling him out of the way. They rolled across rocks and dirt, finally slamming into a stand of trees at the edge of the woods. Jay felt his breath getting knocked out of him.

The cycle hissed in fury and turned towards them. It revved up its engine, kicking up dirt as its wheel span. It almost seemed to be savouring the victory it was about to win. Zane and Cole were too far away to help. It looked like this was the end.

Just before the cycle was about to strike, Jay saw movement out of the corner of his eye. Was it the Fangpyre attacking? No, it was Nya. She was running at top speed, jumping through the air towards the battle. Halfway there, she began to do mid-air somersaults. Each somersault dropped her down close to one of the cycles. Jay saw her hand flash too fast to follow, but he couldn't tell what she was doing.

She landed easily on both feet, hands raised for combat. But there was nothing more to fight. The four cycles stopped in their tracks and toppled over with a loud crash. Nya relaxed and a grin came to her lips.

"Nothing to it," she said.

The four ninja rushed over to her. "What did you do?" asked Jay.

Nya reached into the pocket of her robe and produced four silver keys. "They were still machines, guys. I turned them off."

Jay looked at her, stunned. Zane nodded. Cole smiled. Kai started walking in a circle, smacking himself on the forehead. "Of course!" he cried. "It was so obvious! Why didn't we think of that?"

"We were kind of busy," Cole replied. "Motorcycles were trying to bite us."

"My only question," said Zane, "is why you did not take action sooner, Nya?"

"I wasn't here," she answered. "I saw a Fangpyre slip out of camp last night, so I followed it. Now I know where their nest is...and I am going with you."

Jay opened his mouth to argue. Then he suddenly stopped and glanced at Cole, who nodded. He looked back at Nya, smiling. "Yes. You are."

# Snake Senses

*All creatures use their abilities to stay alive – and this includes snakes. But snakes are also predators, so they use their unique abilities to hunt too.*

## Eyesight

Snake vision varies greatly, from only being able to distinguish light from dark to being very, very sharp. Most species have sharp enough eyesight to track movements. Generally, vision is best in tree snakes and weakest in burrowing snakes. Poor eyesight is not a big problem for snakes as their other senses more than make up for it. Besides, snakes hunt mostly at night.

## Smell and Taste

By flicking out their tongues, snakes collect scents and small particles from whatever they touch, and from the air or water around them. The particles are then passed to a special sensory spot in the mouth called the *Jacobson's organ*, where they are processed. The tongue gives snakes a sort of sense of smell and taste at the same time, and helps them to find out who or what might be nearby.

## Vibration Sensitivity

Snakes of all species can sense other creatures approaching by detecting the faintest vibrations in the air and on the ground. The part of a snake's body that remains in direct contact with the ground is equipped with many special receptors that are incredibly sensitive to vibration. With this ability, snakes can also determine danger or the size of their prey from a great distance.

## Infrared Sensitivity

*Pit vipers*, *pythons*, *rattlesnakes* and some *boas* have receptors that are sensitive to infrared radiation. Some snake species have them in deep grooves between the nostrils and eyes, or in a pit in their upper lip just below the nostrils. Thanks to this infrared sensitivity, these snakes can actually 'see' the radiated heat of warm-blooded animals. This means hunting is very easy for them – no matter if it is day or night.

# Sensei Wu asks

*Cobras have an excellent ear for music. This is why they love to dance to the sound of a snake charmer's flute. True or false?*

**Answer:** False. Cobras are stone deaf, like other snakes. The only thing the cobra dance shows is the snake charmer's smart tricks. To begin the show, the snake charmer stamps his foot. The snake senses the vibration and, alerted, raises its body. The charmer then moves his flute to the rhythm of the music and the cobra simply follows its movement.

# Snake Facts

*What if destiny holds for you an encounter with a snake? Remember these facts well! One day this knowledge may come in very handy...*

**1.** Snakes can eat prey three times as big as their mouths, as they have tendons that can stretch to this size. So it is wise to avoid large snakes!

**2.** *Boa constrictors* or *reticulated pythons* can gobble big animals and go without food for months. So if you stumble across such a snake, there's a good chance it will not be hungry.

**3.** The *king cobra* is one of the most dangerous snakes in the world. Its venom is not very toxic, but it injects it several times in one bite, so the result may be lethal.

**4.** It is easy to identify the *king cobra* because of its characteristic hood, which it spreads when it finds itself in danger. This is a warning – if you don't back away, it will bite you to protect itself.

**5.** Non-venomous snakes – such as pythons – have fangs just like venomous snakes. Just because they don't have venom, it doesn't mean their bite won't hurt!

**6.** It may be hard to believe this unusual snake fact, but these scary creatures are actually very shy of humans and never attack them unless they feel threatened. So don't scare them!

## Sensei Wu asks

*If your enemy has an advantage in size, strength or number, fighting is not a wise option. Some snake species can 'play dead' to put off attackers. True or false?*

**Answer:** True. The hognose, the grass snake and the spitting cobra will fake death when feeling threatened. They flip onto their backs, open their mouths, let their tongues flop out···and produce a terrible smell to make sure that nobody would want to eat them!

**39**

# Ninja Quiz

*It is time to take a break from your adventures and test your memory. Think carefully before deciding upon the correct answer to each question in this quiz.*

1. What sound did Kai awake to in his terrible dream?

2. Who was the first person that Kai saw in the dream?

3. What did Kai do when he saw his transformed friends?

4. Who woke up Kai from his nightmare?

5. Who did Kai fight at the beginning of the other story?

6. How many fights did Kai win in that training session?

7. What kind of vehicles did Jay build for the team?

8. What was it that made Nya feel sad and angry?

9. What problem did the ninja have with the vehicles?

10. Who finally saved the ninja from trouble?

**Answer:** 1. The hissing of a snake, 2. Sensei Wu, 3. He ran to the nearest village for help. 4. Jay, 5. Jay, 6. Three, 7. Motorcycles, 8. There was no vehicle for her, 9. After being bitten by a Fangpyre, the vehicles attacked them, 10. Nya.

# Ninja Quiz

*Now, my young ninja, test your memory before you jump to another adventure. There is only one good answer to each question in this quiz.*

1. How did Zane know that the farming village was in danger?

2. What did the ninja see when they came to the village?

3. What strange thing did the ninja notice on the fruit stand?

4. Who first said out loud that the villagers were hypnotized?

5. What did Zane ride on into the village?

6. What did Jay ask Zane to do for him in the other story?

7. As well as brave, what else did Zane want Jay to be?

8. What did Jay do before Zane could finish the hypnosis?

9. How did Jay get down from the top of the mountain?

10. Who ordered the Hypnobrai to retreat from the village?

**Answer:** 1. A black falcon in his dream told him. 2. The villagers going about their lives. 3. There was only tinned fruit and some rotten fruit. 4. Cole. 5. A wagon loaded with ice. 6. He wanted Zane to hypnotize him. 7. Sensible and cautious. 8. He ran to save a nearby village. 9. He surfed down on a branch of a tree. 10. Lloyd Garmadon.

# Contents

# New Menace to Ninjago

With Lord Garmadon gone, peace had fallen upon Ninjago. But with no enemy to defeat, my ninja became lazy and neglected their Spinjitzu training. I warned them that they must stay sharp, as one day a new enemy would threaten our world. How right I was proved to be, when evil itself unlocked a mysterious snake tribe...

# Snake Eyes

The Hypnobrai are one of the five ancient evil Serpentine tribes that had been banished from Ninjago for centuries. Lloyd Garmadon, my evil brother's son, found their tomb and released them. With their ability to control their enemies' minds using their rattling tails and hypnotic eyes, the Hypnobrai proved a useful ally. Soon, they became Lloyd's army. But although they obeyed him, their own thirst for revenge on Ninjago was growing ever greater.

# Cold Reception

The four ninja walked cautiously down the main street of the village. Their hands hovered over their golden weapons, ready for any trouble that might come their way. So far, though, all was quiet.

"Everything seems fine here," said Jay, looking around. "Are you sure you got the message right, Zane?"

The Ninja of Ice nodded. "The black falcon in my dream said the Hypnobrai were menacing this village. I don't understand why there is no sign of trouble."

Kai looked around. The small farming village looked like every other one he had ever seen: a collection of houses, a general store, an inn, an ice house for storing meat, and lots of very busy people going about their lives. There was certainly no sign of any Hypnobrai here.

"Maybe we shouldn't be listening to a bird from your dreams," he said.

"Welcome, friends," interrupted one of the villagers, a tall, thin man with a short beard. "What brings you to our village?"

Cole stepped forward. "We … um … have you seen any armed snakes sneaking around here?"

The other ninja thought the man would laugh, or maybe even get upset at the suggestion that the Serpentine were around. Instead, his face just went blank. He stared over Cole's head as he said, "Snakes? No, there are no snakes here. There have never been snakes here."

"Okay, that's just weird," Kai whispered to Zane.

"Hey, guys, over here!" said Jay. He was standing near a roadside fruit stand. As the ninja approached, they saw that there was no fresh fruit on display. All they could see was tinned fruit and some apples and oranges that were mostly rotten.

"Whoever heard of a farming community with no fresh fruit?" asked Zane.

"Maybe it's all being used for something else," Jay said quietly. "Spread out. Let's see what we can find."

The four ninja spent the next hour wandering through the town, talking to whoever they could find. Everywhere they went, it was the same:

people would be nice and friendly until they were asked about the Hypnobrai, at which point they started acting like zombies.

When the team got back together, Cole said what they were all thinking. "This whole town has been hypnotized. My guess is they are turning whatever they grow over to the Hypnobrai."

"Why?" asked Kai.

"Snakes have to eat too," shrugged Cole. "This is their supply station while they're raiding other villages."

"What can we do about this?" asked Zane.

"Simple," answered Jay. "We become farmers."

* * *

Later, the four ninja, disguised in farmers' hats, joined the villagers in picking fruit off the trees. As Jay had suspected, the mesmerized locals didn't notice four new faces in the fields. They were focused on gathering fruit for their Serpentine masters.

After several hours' work in the hot sun, the fruit baskets were full. The villagers picked them up and carried them off towards the largest house in town. Kai slipped away from the group and peeked through the side windows of the house. Sure enough, Skales and four Hypnobrai warriors were inside, collecting the crop.

"I think we should interrupt their lunch," said Kai.

"I agree," said Cole. "Hey, where's Zane?"

"He was here a second ago," said Jay. "Do we wait for him?"

"No," said Cole. "Let's take them!"

The three ninja crashed through the windows of the house. The hissing Hypnobrai advanced, ready to fight. Using Spinjitzu, the ninja whirled through the central room of the house, scattering furniture and snakes alike. When they stopped spinning, they found that Skales was still standing. Other Hypnobrai were slithering down from upstairs and up from the basement to join the fight. The ninja were badly outnumbered.

"Get ready for more Spinjitzu," said Cole. "We'll break out and fight them outside. We need room to manoeuvre."

Just then, the ninja heard the sound of glass breaking. A big chunk of ice struck Skales on the side of the head. The Hypnobrai leader hissed angrily.

This was followed by more ice, hurled at high velocity into the house. The hail of frozen missiles drove the snakes back. Kai glanced out of the broken window and saw Zane on top of a wagon loaded with ice from the ice house.

"Come on!" yelled Kai, leading his two friends outside. They joined Zane, grabbing pieces of ice and throwing them at the oncoming Hypnobrai.

"I should have thought of this," said Cole. "Snakes hate ice and snow. It slows them down."

"Then this should stop them . . . cold," said Zane, Shurikens of Ice in hand. He threw the golden weapons and hit two of the snakes, instantly freezing them solid.

"Esssscape!" cried Skales. "We will sssssmashh these ninja another day."

As the Hypnobrai made their escape, the villagers began to snap out of their trances. Deciding it would take too long to explain what had just happened, Cole and the other three ninja slipped back to camp. There would be another day, and another battle, but for now, the village was safe.

# What are Snakes?

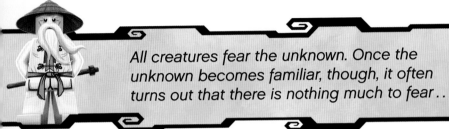

*All creatures fear the unknown. Once the unknown becomes familiar, though, it often turns out that there is nothing much to fear...*

1. Snakes belong to a large animal group called *reptiles*. Reptiles are one of the oldest groups of animals living on Earth – a group which also included dinosaurs millions of years ago.

2. Snakes are cold-blooded animals that change their body temperature to match their surroundings. They raise it by lying in the sun and lower it by slithering into shade.

3. Snakes are predators. Some of them are hunters while others will lie in wait to ambush their prey. But they have enemies, too – the most dangerous being humans.

**4.** Snakes can have a very varied diet. They usually live on small mammals, birds, fish, eggs or insects, and sometimes they even eat each other! And they don't chew – they just swallow their food whole.

**5.** Most snakes hatch from soft, leathery eggs. Some mother snakes find safe and warm places to lay eggs, while others – like the *king cobra* – build nests. Some species, such as boas and rattlesnakes, give birth to live young.

**6.** There are more than 3,000 species of snake in the world. They can be found almost anywhere on land or in water, but they like a warm climate and can't survive in places where the ground stays frozen all year round.

## Sensei Wu asks

*Being reptiles, snakes are close relatives of crocodiles, frogs, lizards, turtles and even dragons. True or false?*

**Answer:** Partly true, but frogs are amphibians, not reptiles, and dragons are mythical creatures that have never really existed (unless you count the Komodo dragon, which is actually a huge lizard that lives in Indonesia!).

# Snakes: Myths and Facts

*Knowledge is precious and ninja are keen learners. However, when a new enemy approaches, it is crucial to be able to tell a fact from a myth.*

## 1. Slimy Snakes

**The Myth:** A snake's skin is disgusting to touch, because it is covered with a slimy substance that makes slithering easier for the snake.

**The Fact:** A snake's skin is dry and mostly smooth. Surprisingly, many people find it pleasant to touch.

## 2. Hypnotizing Eyes

**The Myth:** Snakes can hypnotize their prey to stop it from escaping.

**The Fact:** There is no evidence that snakes are able to do this. It is possible that small animals may become frozen with fear at the approach of a snake.

### 3. Legendary Hoop Snakes

**The Myth:** In order to catch prey, a hoop snake grabs its own tail in its mouth, forms a "hoop" with its body and rolls like a wheel at a great speed.

**The Fact:** There are no hoop snakes in the world. Snakes can be quite fast, but they can't move in this way.

### 4. Ready, Coil, Strike!

**The Myth:** Snakes can strike only from a coiled position. If you see a coiling snake, you can expect an attack.

**The Fact:** Snakes are extremely agile and they move very quickly. If threatened, they can and will strike from any position.

## Sensei Wu asks

*Counting the rattles on a rattlesnake's tail is a good way of telling the snake's age, because this species grows one rattle a year. True or false?*

**Answer: False.** Rattlesnakes add a rattle each time they shed their skin – and they shed it several times a year. Furthermore, rattles may sometimes break off. Therefore, counting them will not tell you a rattlesnake's age.

21

# The Bravest Ninja of All

"Come on, Zane," Jay pleaded. "You have to do this for me."

Zane, the Ninja of Ice, shook his head emphatically. "No. You know Sensei Wu would never approve. Besides, what if something went wrong?"

"Nothing will," Jay said, smiling. "When do you ever make a mistake?"

Zane glanced skyward as he sifted through his memories. "Well, there was the time I let the marshmallows burn in the campfire . . . and the time I laughed inappropriately at one of Kai's stories, thinking it was a joke when it wasn't . . . oh, and the time I took the Sensei's instruction to 'jump to it' as meaning I should jump everywhere all day . . . plus the . . ."

"Okay, I get it!" Jay interrupted. "You can be a real idiot sometimes, does that make you feel better? But you won't mess this up. So please do it."

Zane frowned. Jay, like the others, had become lazy when it came to training. Since the end of the battle with the evil Lord Garmadon, the ninja had faced few challenges. They had become soft. Now Jay's parents were coming to visit and he wanted a short cut to get back to his former level of skill.

"Hypnotize me," Jay said. "You can make me think I am the bravest, toughest, most well-trained ninja ever. And if I *believe* that, I will *be* it. Understand?"

What Zane understood was that his friend was not going to leave him alone until he agreed. Reluctantly, Zane said, "Okay, Jay. We will try it. But I make no promises that it will work."

"Great!" said Jay. "What do I do?"

"Sit down on the ground," Zane answered. He took one of the golden Shurikens of Ice from his robe. "Now watch the shuriken. See how it gleams in the sunlight? Just keep your eyes on it as I move it from side to side. That's right... watch the shuriken and relax, Jay."

It didn't take long to put Jay into a trance. As soon as Zane was sure he was under hypnosis, he said, "Now,

Jay, listen carefully. Believe what I say. Of all the ninja who have ever been, you are the bravest..."

"Zane! Jay! Come quick!" It was Kai, waving his arms frantically. "The Hypnobrai are attacking a nearby village. We have to go!"

"But I..." Zane began. He needed to finish his work with Jay to make sure his friend would be sensible and cautious, as well as brave. This was the worst possible time for an alert.

It was also too late. Jay's eyes snapped open and he jumped to his feet. Zane knew Jay was really still in a trance, even if it wouldn't be obvious to others. The really bad news was that he saw himself as the bravest ninja ever now.

"Jay, wait!" Zane called. But Jay was already snatching up his Nunchucks of Lightning and racing for the village.

By the time Zane caught up with him, he was standing with Kai and Cole. "The problem we have is that there is only one road into the village, and the snakes are guarding it," said Cole. "The only other way in is over a mountain and it's impossible to climb. So we will have to take our chances with the road."

"Nothing is impossible!" Jay said loudly. "I'll climb the mountain, clear the road, and you can march right in."

Before Cole could say anything, Jay was off. Zane hurried to catch up. "Jay, aren't you afraid you might fall off the mountain?"

"Me?" Jay replied. "I'm not afraid of anything!"

"I know," Zane muttered to himself. "That's what I'm afraid of."

The mountain rose hundreds of feet in the air, and Cole was right: only a crazy person would try to climb it . . . crazy, or way too brave for his own good. Jay looked up at the sheer face of rock, then walked over and broke a branch off a nearby tree. He lashed the branch to his back with a short length of rope. Then, despite the fact that there was nothing that even looked like a foothold on the entire mountainside, Jay started to scale the peak.

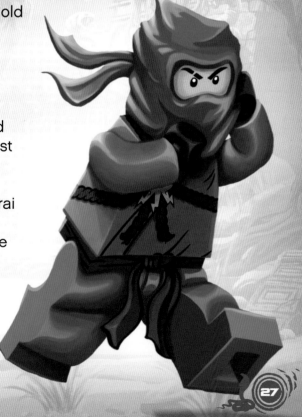

"Be careful!" said Zane, trying his best to follow.

"Let the Hypnobrai be careful," Jay answered, his voice full of confidence. "Not that it will help them once I get there."

*Sensei Wu is not going to be happy*, thought Zane. *I am looking at two straight days of crying lotus push-ups, I think … unless he's really angry, and then it will be one-handed crying lotus push-ups.*

With no fear to slow him down, Jay soon made it to the top of the mountain. He even did a little dance at the peak, while watching Zane struggle to make it up. "Come on, slowcoach," Jay laughed. "We have snakes to smash."

After what felt like forever, Zane made it to the summit. Looking down, he could see the mountain was just as steep on the other side. Far below, the town was visible, with Hypnobrai storming through the central square. They seemed to be going in and out of a big warehouse at the base of the mountain, carrying small crates.

"Lloyd Garmadon, our old foe's son, must have the Hypnobrai stealing for him again," said Zane. "But how are we going to get down there? And how do I know I will hate your answer, Jay?"

With a broad smile, Jay pulled the tree branch off his back. "Here you go. I'll just ride this right down the side of the mountain."

"You can't do that!" exclaimed Zane. "You'll get hurt – or worse!"

"Nothing to worry about," Jay assured him. "See you at the bottom!"

With that, Jay hopped on the tree branch and started surfing down the side of the mountain. Zane knew that even if his friend survived the trip down, he wouldn't survive the crash at the bottom. *I got him into this mess,* thought the Ninja of Ice. *Now I have to get him out.*

Zane dived head-first off the top of the mountain. As he gained ground on Jay, he took out his Shurikens of Ice. He hurled one of them past Jay so that it struck the rocky slope up ahead of the two ninja. Instantly, the rock froze over and the ice curved upward. As Jay hit that spot, he found himself soaring straight up into the sky. Soon he was out of control and falling back toward the mountain.

Before he could hit the rock, Zane slammed into him. Now both ninja were falling toward the warehouse at incredible speed. Zane tossed the second shuriken, creating a spiraling ice slide in front of them. The two hit the slide and rode it down. They were still going way too fast when they reached the bottom. Zane and Jay were hurled off the ice slide and right through the roof of the warehouse.

They landed in the middle of a dozen Hypnobrai and Lloyd Garmadon himself. Zane knew they were in big trouble as more of the snakes poured into the building from outside. Things got even worse when Jay lifted his head from the floor, said, "Huh? Where am I?" and promptly fell unconscious.

Zane sprang to his feet, ready to fight. Just then, he heard a commotion from outside. The doors of the warehouse burst open and Cole and Kai appeared, battling their way through the Hypnobrai warriors. "Thanks for the distraction," said Cole. "Next time, try something a little less insane."

The battle did not last long. As much as Lloyd Garmadon hated the ninja, he didn't want to see his Hypnobrai defeated. He ordered a retreat and the snakes reluctantly slithered off into the woods. While Kai and Cole helped Jay back to camp, Zane started the long climb to retrieve his two shurikens. Once he had done that, he knew he had one more task to perform.

* * *

BLACK
SMITHS

Jay and Zane sat facing each other in the middle of
camp. Zane had once more succeeded in putting Jay
into a trance, and hoped that this time they wouldn't
be interrupted.

"When I count to three, Jay, you will be the bravest
ninja of all," said Zane, "because you will be able to face
your parents just as you are. Do you understand?"

"Yes," said Jay, eyes half-closed.

"One . . . two . . . three," said Zane, clapping his hands
on the last word.

Jay's eyes opened all the way. He took a deep breath and smiled. "Did it work?"

"Well, we saved the village," Zane answered. "Tell me — how do you feel about your parents' visit?"

"Why, not nervous at all anymore," Jay said happily. "Come on, you know me, Zane. It takes more than that to scare me!"

"I know," answered Zane. "Oh, how I know . . ."

# Bite or Hug?

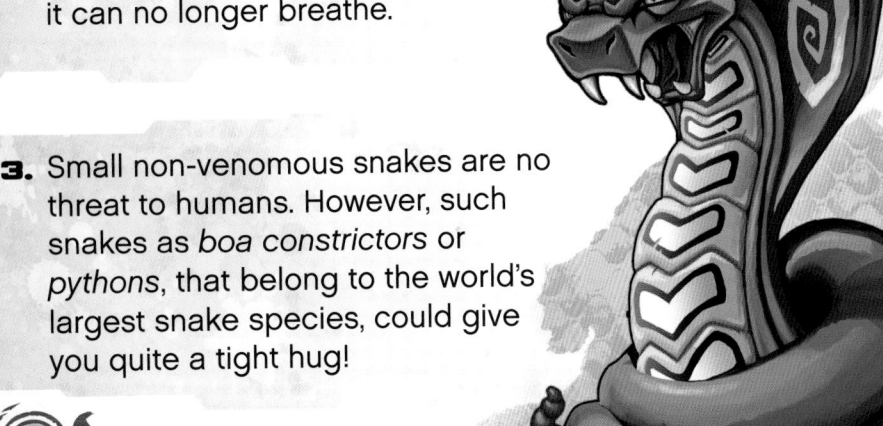

*Victory in combat depends on understanding the opponent's strengths. It always helps to know what kind of danger you are dealing with...*

**1.** Most snakes in the world are non-venomous. Those that have venom use it primarily to immobilize their prey or take its life rather than for self-defence.

**2.** Non-venomous snakes either swallow prey alive or coil themselves around it – like constrictor snakes do – and squeeze the creature until it can no longer breathe.

**3.** Small non-venomous snakes are no threat to humans. However, such snakes as *boa constrictors* or *pythons*, that belong to the world's largest snake species, could give you quite a tight hug!

**4.** Some snake species are very dangerous to humans because their venomous bite can cause painful injury or even loss of life. There are more than 700 venomous snake species in the world.

**5.** All sea snakes are venomous. In fact, they are thought to be the most venomous of all snakes. Luckily, their fangs are quite short and they are unable to bite through an ordinary diver's suit very easily.

**6.** There are some venomous snakes called *spitting cobras* that can eject venom from their fangs. The sprayed venom is harmless to intact skin, but it can cause blindness if it gets into the eye!

# Sensei Wu asks

*The spitting cobras not only aim quite badly but they cannot spit their venom far. True or false?*

**Answer:** So very false! The spitting cobra's spit range is almost two metres. Unfortunately for the one being spat at, this snake has near-perfect aim, and will fire straight into the eyes of its prey.

# Ninja Meets Snake

Knowledge and common sense keep ninja from taking any unnecessary risks. Follow my teachings to survive a meeting with a Serpentine warrior!

## 1. Be invisible

Upon seeing an enemy, ninja do their best to remain unseen. When confrontation is unavoidable, surprise will always be the ninja's advantage.

## 2. Be patient

Ninja take time to observe the opponent from a safe distance. Rushing into action without examining the situation often ends up getting you into trouble.

## 3. Be smart

A different tactic is required for each Serpentine tribe. Ninja must not look into the eyes of a Hypnobrai rattling his tail, or they get hypnotized and become his slaves.

## 4. Be cautious

Ninja never trust a snake. Even Serpentine who seem friendly and harmless can be deceitful and extremely dangerous upon direct contact.

## 5. Be predictive

Ninja evaluate their chances of victory. Calling upon fellow ninja for support might pay off – friends can watch each other's backs when things turn bad.

## 6. Be reasonable

Ninja never attempt an attack when the enemy outnumbers them. There is no shame in withdrawing to safety – it is proof of wisdom, not cowardice.